CLOCKWORK
MOUSE
IN TROUBLE

Pictures by Sally Holmes

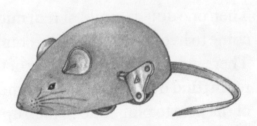

CARNIVAL

There were a great many toys in Billy's playroom. There were big and little dolls, engines, bricks, bears, toy animals – and a clockwork mouse. The clockwork mouse was a merry little fellow. He had a key in his side and when he was wound up he ran all over the place as fast as could be, just like a real mouse. Everyone loved him. Then one day a family of real mice came to live behind the playroom wall. There was a hole in the corner of the room, and at night the mice came out of the hole to play, and to pick up any crumbs that Billy had dropped on the floor.

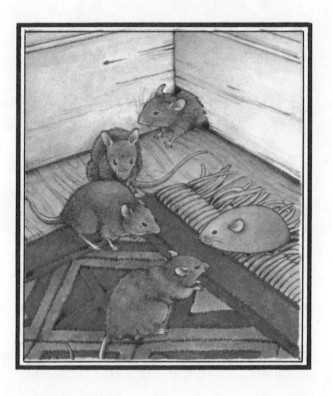

But the dolls didn't like the mice at all.
They pretended that they were afraid
of them. They had once seen Mummy
jump out of her chair, and heard her
squeal loudly when she saw a mouse –
so they thought it was the right thing
to do.

The little clockwork mouse was cross.
"Why are you so silly about my
friends?" he said to the big dolls.
"Those mice won't hurt you. They are
dear little things. You are being silly."

"You are not to talk to us like that," said the biggest doll, called Angelina. "We don't like those mice. We shall chase them out of the playroom every time they come."

So, whenever the real little mice popped their heads out of their hole, the big dolls ran at them, and chased them back. Angelina banged the mother-mouse on the nose with a spoon, and the mother-mouse squealed with pain.

"How unkind you are!" said the clockwork mouse, angrily. "You know they are my friends.

And you know, too, that they don't have very much to eat because the carpet is swept so carefully every day there is hardly ever a crumb left for the mice. And the cupboard door is kept shut so that not even the smallest mouse can get in."

"A good thing, too," said Angelina, unkindly. "Perhaps if they can't find any food here, they will go."

"But I don't want them to go," said the clockwork mouse with tears in his eyes. "They are my friends. It is true that I am only clockwork and they are real, but still I think mouse thoughts, and understand mouse ways, so I am very happy to have them here."

"I shall chase them away every time they come," said Angelina. And she kept her word. She even got the panda to stand by the hole with a little watering-can to pour water on them when they came out.

One of the baby mice was soaked, and he got a bad cold. The clockwork mouse was very upset.

"If you won't let my friends come into the playroom I shall have to go and see *them* down in their hole," he said. "Tonight I will go. I dare say I may find it a bit hard to squeeze through the hole, because I am fat – but I expect I can manage."

He got stuck half-way in the hole but
the other mice managed to pull him
through all right. They were delighted
to see him, especially the little mouse
with a cold.

"I'm sorry we can't offer you any
food," said the mother-mouse, "but
except for a bit of baconrind one of us
found down in the kitchen we haven't
had anything to eat for a day or two."

The clockwork mouse had a lovely
time down in the hole. He gave his key
to the baby mouse who had a cold, and
let him play with it. The mouse was
pleased.
The little mice took the clockwork
mouse down all their holes, and
showed him how they got about
behind the wall.

They met other mice, who were not very pleased to see them.

"You see, we each live behind a different room," said the mother-mouse, "and we are supposed to get our food out of that room – not out of any other. Each family of mice has its own room – but, oh dear, the playroom is not a very good room to have, because it is kept so very clean. We thought it would be a splendid room to run out in and pick up bits and pieces – but except on Sundays when the floor isn't swept, we don't find anything!"

The clockwork mouse enjoyed his
visit. He heard the panda calling down
the hole, and he knew it was time to go.
"Clockwork mouse! It will soon be
morning. You must come back at
once!" called the Panda.
"Good-bye," said the mouse. "I must
go. I will come again tomorrow."

He ran up the passage to the hole in the
playroom wall. He ran across the floor
to the toy cupboard, got into it,
cuddled among the toys and fell
asleep.

The next night he wanted to go and see
his mouse-friends – but he couldn't
move. His clockwork had run down.
He needed to be wound up again.

He called the panda.
"Panda! Wind me up, will you?"
The toys often wound up the
clockwork mouse when he needed it.
The panda came to him to turn his key
and wind him up.
"Why, clockwork mouse, where's your
key?" he asked in surprise. "It isn't in
the hole in your side."
"No, it isn't," said the toys, standing
round and staring. "Have you lost it?"
"Oh, tails and whiskers, I know what
I've done with it!" said the clockwork
mouse, in a fright. "I lent it to the baby
mouse to play with and I forgot to ask
him for it back. So he has still got it,
down the mouse-hole!"

"Good gracious!" said Angelina.
"Whatever will you do?"
"He'd better go down the mouse-hole
and get it," said the panda. Angelina
gave a sniff.

"How very, very silly you are, panda! If the clockwork mouse can't run because he isn't wound up, *how* can he go and fetch his key?"

"I didn't think of that," said the panda, and he would have blushed red, if only he could. "Well, perhaps the mice will come out of their hole tonight and bring back the key."

"No, they won't," said the mouse sadly. "You see, they are afraid to come out now, panda, ever since you stood outside with that watering-can."

The panda felt ashamed. "Angelina told me to do that," he said. Then Angelina felt ashamed, too, and very sorry. It would be dreadful if the little clockwork mouse, whom they all loved, should never be able to run again, because his key was down a mouse-hole and couldn't be got back. The mice didn't come out of the hole with the key. They were too afraid – and besides, they felt sure that their clockwork friend would never have left his key behind if he were going to need it so soon.

Everyone in the playroom was upset.
"This is dreadful," said the fat teddy
bear. "Why did we scare those mice
away? Now we have brought
unhappiness to the clockwork mouse
we love. There he lies, in the toy
cupboard, not able to run about, or
play games or anything. Angelina, it
is mostly your fault this happened.
Just think of some plan, please!"

So Angelina thought and thought, and
at last an idea came.
"We are all too big to go down the
mouse-hole," she said. "I couldn't
possibly get down, and neither could
you, panda. And certainly fat Teddy
couldn't. But I know who could."
"Who?" said everyone.
"The three doll's house dolls," said
Angelina.
"They are very tiny."

So the panda called out the three doll's house dolls from their dear little house, and spoke to them.

"Tiny dolls, will you go down the mouse-hole and get the clockwork mouse's key for him?"

"We are afraid," said the tiny dolls.

"There is nothing to be afraid of," said Angelina. "I only pretended to be afraid of the mice. I was silly. You go, tiny dolls – and as a reward you shall use the little stove in your doll's house for cooking! You have always wanted to, and we have never let you because we were afraid you might set the house on fire. But the panda can fill his watering-can with water and stand by to see that nothing gets on fire."

Now the doll's house dolls had always wanted to cook on their little stove. It was such a good stove. They looked at one another in joy.

"All right," they said. "We will go down the mouse-hole and fetch the key."

"And tell the mice they can safely come into the playroom," said Angelina. "Tell them we are sorry we scared them away. We will be kind to them now."

So the three doll's house dolls, holding hands tightly went down the mouse-hole. The mice were very surprised to see them, and very sorry to know that the clockwork mouse missed his key so much.

The baby mouse gave it up at once. The three doll's house dolls loved him. He was really sweet.

"Angelina is going to let us cook on our little stove," they told the mice. "We shall make cakes and puddings. If you will bring the baby mouse to see us when his cold is better we will give you each a cake."

Well, wasn't that lovely! The mice beamed with delight and promised to come. Then up the passage back to the hole went the doll's house dolls, feeling quite excited with their adventure. The mouse was soon wound up again, and didn't he rush up and down the carpet with joy! "You will need winding up *again* silly," said the panda.

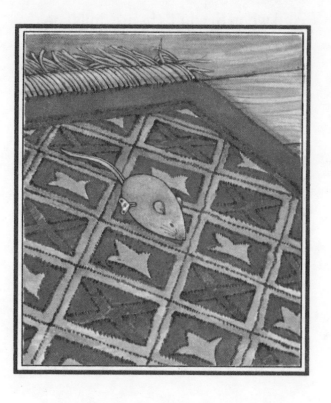

Now the real little mice come into the playroom every night and play, and nobody minds them, not even Angelina.

And when the doll's house dolls cook on their little stove, the little mice run into the kitchen there at once – and so does the clockwork mouse too. They each have a cake or a bit of pudding – and don't they enjoy it, all sitting happily together round the kitchen table.

I *would* like to see them, wouldn't you?